I0737178

BURNING THE HELP

LATRESA RICE

WORKBOOK PRESS LLC
187 E Warm Springs Rd,
Suite B285, Las Vegas, NV 89119, USA

Website: https://workbookpress.com/
Hotline: 1-888-818-4856
Email: admin@workbookpress.com

Ordering Information:
Quantity sales. Special discounts are available on quantity purchases by corporations, associations, and others. For details, contact the publisher at the address above.

Library of Congress Control Number:
ISBN-13:   978-1-958176-09-2 (Paperback Version)
                978-1-958176-10-8 (Digital Version)

REV. DATE: 09/29/2023

BURNING THE
HELP

Latresa Rice

CONTENTS

INTRODUCTION

There comes a time when, "Aww she's so cute! I can't wait to watch her! You can call me anytime," turns into "ring, ring… no answer."

Have you ever watched anyone else's children for them? Why did you agree to watch them? Do you feel burned out from doing so? I have been there. As a result, I want to help parents avoid placing themselves in the position of failing to have adequate support for their children.

Many people write books about parenting techniques, offering their opinions and advice. However, we rarely see books written by the babysitter that shares advice to help parents find and keep great childcare assistance. Where is the voice of the babysitter that used to love watching other people's children, and then suddenly, they no longer have the desire to do so? What happened? Why doesn't anyone want to help these parents out by watching their children? What can parents do to rebuild this connection once it has been broken? Are there any other resources available to help them?

In this engaging book titled, "Burning the Help," which is written from the perspective of a previously burned-out babysitter, you will learn some of the things that parents do that burn out their support network, and techniques to extinguish the flames once they have started burning.

You will also have access to a list of resources that you can contact to get adequate support if you have burned your help and cannot douse the flames in enough time to avoid destroying your support system. It takes a village to raise exceptional members of our society. Everyone should do their best to avoid burning it.

CHAPTER 1

I'm In Love

"Ring! Ring! Ring! Ring!" was the sound that Helen heard at 9:00 am on a Saturday morning when she was preparing to make peach cobbler infused pancakes, cheese eggs, and sausage linksfor breakfast.

In response to the call, she ran from her Italian-themed kitchen to her dining room table to answer the phone. Her heart was beating fast, and she was breathing rapidly as she picked up the receiver.

"Hello?" Helen asked, breathlessly.

"Helen! Guess what?" Ariel asked, excitedly.

"What? Girl, tell me!" Helen demanded.

"Ashanti just had her baby at Hope Field Hospital! It's a girl! They are both ok," Ariel added.

Excited and puzzled, Helen asked, "Where is Hope Field Hospital?"

"It's in Detroit off Woodward by John R Road," Ariel explained.

"I'm here with her now, but I must go to work. Are you coming?" Ariel asked.

"Yes! I can't wait to meet the little princess!" Helen answered without hesitation.

"I'm on my way!"

Immediately, Helen hung up the phone, dashed into her kitchen to put away all the ingredients for her unmade breakfast, grabbed a bagel and orange juice, and ran out the door. Then, she jumped into her car and drove to the hospital.

"I wonder who this little angel looks like? I know she is so cute! I can't wait to hold her. I love her already!" Helen thought, as she drove her metallic midnight blue 2020 S Class Mercedes Benz to the hospital.

Knowing that hospitals don't allow parents to take their babies home without a car seat, Helen stopped at Save-Mart to purchase a combination car seat and stroller for Ashanti's new bundle of joy, then continued on her journey to the hospital.

"Yes! A close parking space just for me! Thank you, Jesus!" Helen shouted, as she parked her car in the hospital parking lot, then entered the building.

Colorful portraits of friendly looking lions, bears, giraffes, and rabbits decorated the brightly colored walls of the hospital.Helen eagerly waited in line to get a visitor's pass so that she could see Ashanti, and the beautiful gift from God.

"Next!" the receptionist yelled.

"Hi. I would like to get a visitor's pass to see Ashanti

Morris," Helen asked the woman at the desk, politely.

"Unfortunately, it is our policy that patients are only allowed to have two visitors at a time. Currently, Ms. Morris already has two visitors in her room," the receptionist explained.

"Feel free to have a seat in the waiting room and I will call your name once someone leaves," she said.

Determined to see her younger sister's baby, and to make sure Ashanti was ok, Helen took a seat in the crowded waiting room next to an elderly woman.

"Sit down!" the elderly woman yelled at the three children who were running around the hospital waiting area playing tag.

"I would love to help you with the children, ma'am. Do you mind if I talk to them?" Helen asked.

"I don't mine. They are my granddaughter's kids. I am so sick of this! She can't even take care of these three and now she is having a fourth child. Lord, help me!" the older woman moaned.

"I'm sorry you are not having a great day," Helen immediately replied.

"Children are such a blessing though, I'm sure she appreciates everything you do to help her. God sees all that you are doing. You will be rewarded by him for the love that you are showing to her and her children," Helen said kindly.

The elderly woman burst into tears, then embraced Helen and said, "Thank you. What are you here in the hospital for?"

"My sister just gave birth to my niece!" Helen replied with great joy.

"Oh that's beautiful. How old is your sister?" asked the elderly lady.

"She's 19 years old and she just graduated from Driver's High School. She received a full-ride scholarship to Hidden Valley University. It is one of the best universities for her because it is well-known for its medical program and she wants to be a doctor," Helen explained.

"She had so much going for her, and just had a baby? Her life is over! That's so sad," the elderly woman said.

Helen was furious. Nobody talks about her family members like that!

With her eyebrows raised and her face twisted into fifty knots, Helen stood up from where she was playing with the children, placed her hand on her hip and said, "Listen lady. I try to respect my elders, but don't come for me or my family unless I send for you. You need to watch your mouth. I don't take kindly to being disrespected or folk disrespecting my family. You have a nice day!" Then, she turned and stormed out of the waiting area.

As Helen was walking away, she heard the receptionist shout, "Helen Morris!"

The thought of seeing her sister and her beautiful niece erased the entire conversation she just had with the bitter elderly lady in the waiting area.

With an exuberant smile on her face, she sashayed towards the counter to acquire her visitor's pass, then walked towards the elevator to go to room C3025.

"Click, click, click, click, click, click," was the sound made by Helen's heels, as she quickly walked through the halls in the hospital towards room C3025.

"Hey, beautiful!" Helen exclaimed, as she walked into her sister's hospital room.

To the left of the door was a sanitizing foam dispenser. Before walking over to the bed where her sister was resting, she placed sanitizing foam on her hands, then sprinted to the bed to hug her sister.

Ashanti smiled and replied with a slow, steady tone of voice, "Hey Sis, thank you for being here. Did you see my baby yet? I just want to hold her, but I am so tired."

"Not yet, Sis. I will go ask the hospital staff how long it's going to take them to bring the baby in here. Be right back, Sis," Helen replied, then she walked out of the room to the nurses' station.

"Excuse me," Helen said loudly.

Hurrying from the back of the room, a nurse rushed to the front desk. "Yes ma'am. How can I help you?" she inquired.

"I'm visiting my sister in room C3025. She said that she still hasn't seen her baby yet. How long will it take before she can see her new baby?" Helen asked.

"Your sister's nurse is cleaning the baby right now. She should be finished within the next 10-15 minutes," the nurse explained.

Helen thanked her for the information, then returned to Ashanti's room.

"Sis, they said you will be able to see her in another 10-15 minutes. Are you ok? Do you need anything?"

"No, I just want to see my baby before I go to sleep. I'm super tired," replied Ashanti.

"I know, Sis. She is coming really soon. Have you thought about what you are going to name her?" asked Helen.

"Tatiana Rose Harper," Ashanti said with a smile.

Trying not to look disgusted at the fact that this angel will have her father's last name, Helen exclaimed, "Tatiana Rose is such a beautiful name sis. I love her already! That's Ti Ti's angel. I can't wait to hold her!"

Ashanti nodded and laid her head on her two pillows as she continued to lie in the hospital bed, awaiting the return of her princess.

Sitting down, Helen thought to herself, "He doesn't deserve to be able to give my niece his last name. He hasn't married my sister, and the whole time that she was pregnant, this clown kept yelling that the baby wasn't his! He is such a poor example of a father. I hope and pray that he grows up and truly takes care of my niece. Maybe my sister will grow up as well, for the sake of Tatiana. Lord, only you know. I place them all in your hands."

Helen's thoughts were interrupted by the presence of a short, stocky, caramel-colored man wearing blue jeans that were hanging below his buttocks, a white t-shirt with his hair braided vertically from his front hairline to the back of his head. It was Ashanti's child's father, Zadel.

"Hey baby girl, I'm back. I wanted to get you some balloons. Did they bring the baby in here yet?" Zadel asked

Ashanti.

"Thanks, baby! Not yet," Ashanti replied.

Helen was sitting in a chair in the far corner of the room trying not to be noticed by him. She didn't want to speak to him at all, but for the sake of her sister she decided to speak to him, if he spoke to her first.

While he was looking at the board to see who the nurse on duty was, Zadel noticed Helen. He said "Oh, hey, Helen. I didn't know that you were here. How are you?"

"Hi Z, I'm good; just waiting to hold my niece," Helen replied with a flat affect and in a monotone voice.

"Straight up! That's cool. Thanks for coming. We appreciate it," Zadel replied.

This awkward conversation was pleasantly interrupted when the doctor and nurses entered the room.

"Here she is!" the nurse announced cheerfully, as she came into the room. She walked to Ashanti's bedside, singing, and rocking Helen's precious niece.

Ashanti eagerly turned towards the nurse and embraced the baby, while Zadel looked at his daughter with amazement and great joy.

Zadel took pictures with his cell phone while Ashanti was holding the baby.

"Baby, do you want to hold her?" Ashanti asked Zadel.

"No, I'll hold her when she gets bigger. I don't want to hurt her," Zadel replied.

"Ok, baby," Ashanti said to Zadel.

"Sis, do you want to hold her?" Ashanti asked Helen.

"Hecky yeah! Give me my angel! How much does she weigh?" Helen inquired.

"She is 7 pounds, 4 ounces, and 14 inches long!" Ashanti exclaimed, as she looked lovingly at Tatiana. "Hi, Mommy's baby," she said, as she passed Tatiana to Helen, in an attempt to get her to smile.

Helen embraced Tatiana and spoke softly to her. After hearing Zadel's phone vibrate, Ashanti turned towards Zadel. She noticed him smiling as he read a text message, biting his bottom lip like he used to do whenever she put on a sexy dress and heels in his presence, before taking her on a date.

"Who the heck is that?" Ashanti asked furiously.

"Why you trippin, bae?" Zadel retorted.

"I see you over there smiling like it's me on the other end

of that phone. Now tell me the truth, Z. Who the heck is that?" Ashanti demanded.

"Nobody! Dang! I can't smile? I just got a job offer and I was happy about it. You always trippin. You know I only want you, bae." Zadel told her.

While still embracing the new baby, Helen turned towards her sister and said, "You need to take it easy, Sis. Are you ok?" Ashanti did not respond.

Helen turned towards Zadel and said "Z, what is going on? Why is she so angry?"

Immediately, the machines went off. Then nurses came into the room to check Ashanti's IV and blood pressure. The nurse asked, "What is going on in this room that is causing her blood pressure to be elevated?

Zadel replied, "Nothing, she just trippin."

Ashanti tearfully screamed, "I hate you! Get out!"

"I'm not going nowhere! Tatiana is my baby too!" Zadel protested.

The nurse turned towards him and said, "Sir, I need you to leave this room for the health of the patient. I apologize, but her blood pressure is continuing to rise the longer you remain in the room. I do not want to have to call security. Please leave, sir."

"Man, whatever! I'm out!" yelled Zadel as he stormed out of the room, then rushed out of the hospital.

"Whine, whine," Tatiana cried.

"Ashanti, I need you to calm down. I don't know what the heck is going on, but the longer you cry, the more upset your baby will be. It's going to be ok, Sis. Nothing is worth putting yourself in harm's way by sending your blood pressure through the roof. Think about Tatiana right now. She needs you to be calm," Helen said to her sister.

Sniffling, Ashanti replied, "You're right, Sis. Can you bring her to me so I can hold her again?"

Helen swiftly carried the baby to Ashanti and placed Tatiana in her arms.

Immediately Tatiana stopped crying when her mother held her close and kissed her on the cheek.

"Mommy loves you, Tatiana. I'm sorry, baby. Muah."

Helen sat back in her chair and continued to watch Ashanti and the baby bonding. At 3:00 pm, Helen said to Ashanti, "I have to leave, Sis. Can I hold her one more time?"

"Sure. Here, Sis" Ashanti replied, as she passed Tatiana

to Helen. Gazing at her niece, she sang the following song to Tatiana:

"That is Auntie's gorgeous baby! Dunt dunt dunt dunt dunt dunt dunt! Muah!"

For the first time, Tatiana opened her eyes and smiled. Helen was so overjoyed! She turned her head to look at her sister, then Helen smiled and excitedly exclaimed, "Sis, she opened her eyes and smiled at me! She loves me! Hashtag, I'm her favorite."

Much to Helen's surprise, Ashanti was sleeping. Helen rocked Tatiana to sleep, then placed her in the baby bed next to Ashanti. She left the room and informed the hospital staff where the new car seat/stroller for the baby was located, so Ashanti would have it before they went home from the hospital. "Then, she travelled from the hospital to StarChucks."

Benefit of the Doubt

"Yes! I made it on time!" Helen thought to herself, arriving at her business meeting 15 minutes early.

Helen walked into Star Chucks carrying her black leather briefcase, containing her manuscript, a notepad, highlighter, calculator, an ink pen, business cards, and a USB drive. She looked around the room for a man wearing a black blazer with a gold 'M' at the top left corner, and the words "Malcolm Publishing" circled around it. Finally, she recognized him sitting three tables away from the entrance reading a newspaper.

She briskly walked to his table and said, "Hello. Are you Malcolm Peterson? I'm Helen Morris," she said, introducing herself. "It's a pleasure to meet you, Sir."

"Hello, yes I am. The pleasure is all mine, Ms. Morris. Please allow me to get your chair for you," Malcolm said pleasantly, as he stood up, pulled out her chair, and waited for her to sit down. Then, he pushed her chair in and returned to his seat. He was approximately six feet and one inch in height, with a caramel complexion, an athletic frame, and perfectly straight teeth. After he flashed that thousand-watt smile at Helen, she was very distracted. She expected to see an older gentleman with gray hair, but God sent her a tall, handsome replica of Himself! Helen looked up at the ceiling, as if God was in position with his hands stretched out waiting for her response to Malcolm's presence, and thought to herself, "Lord, help me get through this business meeting without making a fool of myself, because this man is fine!"

"Would you like a pastry or anything to drink?My treat," Malcolm offered, smiling at Helen.

"Um, sure. I would love a glass of water and a cheese Danish," replied Helen.

"Coming right up!" Malcolm said.

While Malcolm approached the counter to purchase the requested items, Helen's phone vibrated. She glanced at it and saw that it was her sister calling from the hospital. She quickly answered her phone.

"Hello!"

"Hey, Sis, can you pick up me and the baby?" Ashanti asked. "We are being discharged from here and her dad is not answering any of my calls," she said.

"Hey. Yes, I can, but I am in a business meeting that isn't over for another hour. I would have to travel from Farmington Hills to Detroit right after the meeting, so I probably wouldn't make it to you until another two hours from now. Can you call Ariel, Momma, or any of your other friends?" Helen asked.

"I don't want to bother Ariel because she is at work. and I didn't call Momma, because I didn't want to hear her mouth about Zadel. You can just pick us up when you get finished," replied Ashanti.

"Ok," Helen said hesitantly. Then, she ended the call.

"One cheese Danish and a cup of water for the lady, and

one of each for me," stated Malcolm, returning to the table.

"Is everything ok, Helen?"Malcolm asked. "I don't see that smile that I saw when you walked in," he added, looking concerned.

"I'm sorry, I was thinking about a phone call that I received a moment ago. I'm back!" Helen replied with a smile.

"Well, since I have the beautiful Ms. Helen Morris' full and undivided attention, let me first say that your book "Heart Brake" was reviewed by our team and they suggested that we would like to publish it, and then submit it as a treatment to consider for film production. I haven't reviewed it yet for final approval," Malcolm informed her, smiling.

"Sounds fantastic! However, I will need more details about what your agency will do for me, regarding the promotion of my book, upon final approval. Assuming that you will be reviewing it soon, can you email me a copy of your book contract within the next few days?" Helen asked.

"Absolutely!" Malcolm replied, and then continued to eat his delectable cheese Danish and drink a sip of water from his cup.

"Great! I look forward to it!" she said excitedly. "Well, Malcolm, as much as I would love to continue this wonderful meeting with you, I have to leave to take care of a family emergency," Helen explained.

"No problem, Ms. Morris. I would like to get a little more information about your background and hear about the creation of such a dynamic book! Is there another day that you would be able to meet with me to discuss your book in more detail?" Malcolm asked.

"Yes. I am typically available Tuesdays and Thursdays," Helen said. "Can we meet next week, Thursday, at 6:00 pm? Same location?"

"It's a date! I mean, I'll see you at Star Chucks next Thursday at 6:00 pm," Malcolm responded quickly with a smile.

Helen laughed and walked out of the coffee shop towards her car, to go pick up her sister and niece from the hospital.

Arriving at the hospital, she noticed that her sister and niece were already waiting in the main lobby.

"Hey, Sis," Ashanti said.

"Hey, Sis. Awww, look at Auntie's angel! Sorry I am running a little behind," Helen said breathlessly. "I left my meeting as soon as I could."

"It's all good. I'm just glad that you could come pick us up. Can you take us to Zadel's house?" asked Ashanti.

In an instant, Helen's starry-eyed trance gazing at her niece turned into a frustrated stare of death at her sister. Helen was so irritated that she shouted, "You've got to be kidding me! Why couldn't he just come pick y'all up?"

"He couldn't pick us up, because he didn't know what time he would get the call to go into work, so he was waiting by the phone," Ashanti explained.

"Waiting by the phone? Seriously?" Helen demanded, fuming. "I was in a business meeting and the father of your child had to wait by the phone at his house, even though he carries a cell phone everywhere he goes? This is ridiculous!" Helen exclaimed, annoyed.

"You don't have to do anything for us since you feel like that. You can just leave! He will pick us up when he can," Ashanti retorted, rolling her eyes at her sister.

"Sis, I will drop you both off over there," Helen said. "I am irritated because you always defend him, even when he is super wrong. You are the mother of his child, and he couldn't arrange for you and the baby to be picked up from the hospital? He couldn't ask someone else to stay by the phone for him until he got back?"

"I don't want to talk about this! I'm tired. Can we just go?" Ashanti said, sounding exhausted.

"Yes, Ashanti. I will go pull the car around, so you won't have to walk too far after they bring you and the baby to the car in a wheelchair.

As Helen was bringing the car to the front, a white Ford F-150 whipped in front of her and out jumped Zadel.

"Zadel, what are you doing here?" demanded Helen.

"Hey, Helen. Ashanti called me earlier to say that she needed me to pick her and the baby up. I told her that I couldn't until I got my phone call, but since I got the call about 15 minutes ago, I decided to come get both of my babies. It's a surprise," Zadel said, with a wink and a smile.

"I don't believe this! What a total waste of my time! You couldn't call her to tell her that you would be able to pick her and the baby up?" Helen said angrily. "I left my meeting early in order to pick them up. I could have continued my business meeting. Tell Ashanti that I am leaving," she retorted, walking briskly back towards her car.

"Ok, I can do that," Zadel replied with a nonchalant tone of voice and facial expression.

"Lord, I am so irritated! I place them in your hands. Please bless the birth of my niece to cause both Zadel and my sister to grow up," Helen prayed, as she drove home.

Helen's Place

After parking her Mercedes Benz in the driveway, Helen unlocked the front door and entered her home. Immediately, she placed her keys on the hook inside of the vestibule. Walking toward her tan-colored leather couch to rest her feet, she noticed a red light blinking on her house phone, indicating that she had new messages. "I wonder who called me," Helen thought to herself, as she picked up the receiver to listen to her voice messages. Much to her surprise, she had five missed messages! Two were from Ashanti, one from Ariel, one from her mother, and one from Malcolm of Malcolm Publishing. Helen pressed play and listened to the following messages:

Message one from phone number 313-675-8920

"Hey, Sis, I know you are mad at me. I'm sorry. I didn't know that he was coming to get us. I tried to call you on your cell phone, but you aren't answering my calls. Can you call me back, please?" Ashanti asked.

Message two from phone number 313-675-8920

"Really Helen? You are still just going to ignore my

calls? I said I'm sorry. What else do you want me to do? I needed some help. As my sister, I thought I could call you, but you are ignoring me as if you don't love me anymore because you have an attitude. Can you just call me back so we can talk?"

Message three from phone number 734-887-3425

"Hey Helen! This is Ariel. I know you are busy loving on your new niece. She is so cute! I hate to bother you, but I really need your help. Can you watch my son for me? Call me back when you get this message. Love you!"

Message four from phone number 313-549-9076

"Helen. This is your mother. I heard about what happened between you and your sister today. I know you are probably upset, but you are the oldest and I am expecting you to fix this. Your sister just had a new baby, and she needs you. Get over yourself and be that beautiful person that I know you are. I love you. Call me when you get this message."

Message five from phone number 734-567-8923

"Hi, Helen. It's Malcolm of Malcolm Publishing. I

was calling to say that I have read the first 10 pages of your manuscript and I'm impressed! Can you call me back so we can schedule a date to discuss your book publishing contract? I'm looking forward to hearing back from you soon! Take care," Malcolm said, then hung up.

"Yes! Let me call Malcolm back first, and then I will call Ariel," Helen thought to herself, as she dialed Malcolm's number.

"Hello, Ms. Morris. Thank you for returning my call. How are you?" Malcolm inquired.

"I've been better, but it's a blessing to still be living," Helen said with a chuckle.

"I completely agree. I hope things turn around for you soon. Did you get a chance to listen to my message?" he asked.

"Yes, it was the highlight of my day! I am so glad that you are enjoying my manuscript," Helen said with great joy.

"I am happy to be the one to put that beautiful smile back on your face with my message. By the time you called me back I had already finished reading your manuscript. It is really good! I love it! Although I can't publish it myself," he admitted.

"I have spoken to Paul of Henderson Publishing," Malcolm continued, "and I asked him to review your manuscript.

After two hours, he called me and said that he read it, and he loves it! His agency would like to publish "Heart Brake." Would you be willing to have Henderson Publishing publish your book?" Malcolm asked.

"Oh, well since they are a good publishing company, I would definitely consider it. Can I ask you a question, though?" Helen inquired.

"Yes. You can ask me anything you like, Ms. Morris," Malcolm answered.

"Because you said you love my manuscript, why are you refusing to publish it? I love your agency and I really wanted your company to publish my book."

"I will definitely answer your question, but first can you answer this question for me? Do you believe in love at first sight?" he asked boldly.

"Yes I do, but I've never experienced it," Helen admitted.

"I do as well. I experienced it the moment I laid eyes on you at Star Chucks. I cannot publish your book, because I am interested in you, and I am the owner of this company. Ms. Morris, would you grant me the privilege of getting to know you better?" he asked.

Helen was speechless. She took the phone receiver

away from her ear, then looked at it with a shocked, yet excited expression and answered, "Yes, Malcolm. And please call me Helen."

Malcolm smiled to himself and said, "Can I take you out to dinner next Saturday night, Helen?"

"Yes. What time works best for you?" she asked quickly.

"6:30 pm. Does that work for you?" he asked.

"Yes. It sounds perfect," Helen replied.

"Great! I will pick you up at 6:30 pm," Malcolm stated.

Puzzled, Helen asked, "Don't you need my address, Sir?"

Malcolm laughed, then answered, "I still have the envelope you sent me with your address on it when you mailed us your manuscript, but you can give it to me again, so I don't feel like a stalker."

Helen laughed, then replied, "No, Stalker. You already have it. I'll see you then!"

"You most certainly will. By the way, what's your favorite color?"

"Blue, gold, and chocolate," Helen answered. "What can I say?" she asked comically, then stated, "I don't have just one favorite color."

"Ha ha ha, I wouldn't expect anything less. You are truly one of a kind, and I look forward to enjoying a delicious meal with you next weekend," Malcolm said warmly. "I have to go now and finish reviewing some other manuscripts, but when would be a good time for me to call you tomorrow?" he asked.

"Anytime between 5:00 and 11:00 pm," Helen replied.

"Excellent. Good night, beautiful. Talk to you tomorrow."

Helen hung up the phone and flopped onto her couch. "I can't believe this is happening to me! Thank you, Lord! This man is fine, rich, loves God, and he is interested in me. What more can a girl ask for?" Helen thought, smiling happily, then dialed Ashanti's number.

"Hello?" Ashanti answered.

"Hey, Ashanti. I'm returning your call. What's up?" Helen asked.

"Nothing now," Ashanti said with an attitude.

"Ok, well, have a good night," Helen said nonchalantly.

Ashanti slammed the phone receiver down, as if it was a piece of steak she was tenderizing.

"She gets on my nerves! How dare she have an attitude when she wronged me!" Helen said angrily, as she walked out of her front room toward her bathroom to shower and prepare for bed.

After exiting the shower, Helen thought to herself, "Sometimes, you just have to wash away all the stress of the day by engaging in selfcare. Today is my day to do so." Then, she put on lavender-colored satin pajamas, laid down in her bed, and drifted off to sleep.

Chapter 2

Missing Items

Helen woke up at 6:00 am the next morning, well-rested from a good night's sleep, and thought to herself, "Oh my goodness! I forgot to call Ariel back! Let me call her now."

"Ring. Ring. Ring!"

"Hey, Helen!" Ariel said.

"What's up, girl?" Helen responded. "Sorry to call you so early, but I wasn't able to call you back sooner. Yesterday, I had a rough day, and after my shower I fell asleep."

"No problem, girl, I totally understand that. I know you're busy, so let me get to the reason that I called you yesterday. Can you watch Shawn for three days, five months from now? I know that it's a ways off, but I would like to ensure that I have a babysitter for him. I want to go to a retreat out of town for the weekend with a few friends from church, and children aren't allowed to attend."

"Girl, yes! I love him! What are the dates you would need me to watch him?" Helen asked.

"I would drop him off at 6:00 pm on Friday, May 22nd, and pick him up by 6:00 pm on Sunday, May 24th. Is that ok for you?"

"Yes, ma'am! See you and my baby on Friday, May 22!"

"Thank you so much, Helen! I appreciate all that you do

for me. I pray that God blesses you with your heart's desires. Love you!" Ariel shouted.

"No problem," Helen said reassuringly. "It will be my pleasure," she added joyfully, and ended the call.

"I still need to call my mom back," Helen mused, "but I really don't want to hear what she has to say about Ashanti's and my issue. She always takes her side, regardless of whether she is right or wrong."

"Actually, you know what?" Helen said out loud. "I'm not calling her back! I'm grown. I don't have to call anyone back that I don't want to call. I pay this phone bill. I'm not calling her back!" Helen muttered to herself, sitting down on the couch.

About a half an hour later, Helen's tough exterior turned into a bed of marshmallows. She moved to the edge of the couch, grabbed the receiver, placed it to her ear, and called her mother.

"Hello," her mother answered in a monotone voice.

"Hi Mom. It's Helen. I was just returning your call."

"I know who this is, but what I don't know is why it took you so long to call me back, girl. I'm still your mother. I'm not pleased to be last on your list of returned phone calls," Helen's mother replied with an attitude.

Helen thought to herself, "Dang! How did she know that

she was last on my list! Is she psychic? She is always reading our minds!" Then, she retorted, "Mom, I was really busy, but I'm on the phone with you now. What did you want to talk about?"

"I told you that in the voicemail Helen, didn't you listen to it?" her mother said, sounding irritated.

Helen looked at the receiver of her phone, rolled her eyes as if she were rolling a pair of dice, then answered, "Yes ma'am. I heard it, and I reached out to Ashanti already."

"Oh good! I love to see my children get along and help each other. I know you didn't want to do it, and you probably think that it's not fair for me to ask you to call her, but you are the oldest, so you have to set an example," Helen's mother said firmly.

"I know, Mom," Helen replied with a sigh.

"Don't use that tone with me, young lady! I will not have you disrespecting me, because you have an attitude," her mother said angrily.

"Mom, I'm not trying to be disrespectful. I'm just tired. I will call you back another day. Ok?" Helen asked.

"Ok, baby girl. Get some rest. Hopefully, your attitude gets better when you wake up. I love you," Helen's mother said, suddenly sounding tranquil.

Placing her hand on her head, Helen reluctantly admitted, "Love you, too."

Pleasant Surprise

"You are the best! Don't let these haters cause you stress," were the words to a song Helen heard when the alarm on her cell phone went off at 6:00 am.

Helen arose expediently, prayed, read her Devotional, worked out for 30 minutes, ate her breakfast, and took a shower.

After she dried off and put on her jasmine-scented lotion, deodorant, clothes, jewelry, perfume, and make-up, her phone rang. She looked at the caller ID and noticed that it was Malcolm calling. She immediately answered the phone.

"Hello," Helen said pleasantly.

"Good morning, beautiful. How are you this morning?" he said in a baritone voice, similar to the singer, Barry White.

"I'm fine. Thank you for the lovely compliment," she answered. "How are you, Malcolm?"

Malcolm was so excited that she knew who he was, that his words fell out of his mouth, like a football falls from the arms of a hit player.

"Well, I, I mean, you know, I'm great," he stammered. "Thank you for asking. I know you are probably busy, but I was just thinking about you, so I decided to call you, just to hear your voice. I actually thought that I would have to hear it on your voicemail, but God so graciously allowed me to hear it directly from you," he declared.

"Awww, that is so sweet. You just made my morning, Sir. Shut your mouth and keep on talking!"Helen said jokingly. "I'm all ears," she added, then the two of them laughed hysterically.

"You are so funny! I love it!" Malcolm said. "I am looking forward to our date, beautiful. I have a meeting to attend in five minutes, so I have to go, but I will definitely call you again later, if that's ok with you?"

"You can call me any time before 11:00 pm. I enjoy speaking with you, Mr. Peterson," Helen replied, smiling.

"Alright, Ms. Morris. I will definitely do that. I am honored to have the opportunity to get to know you, my queen," Malcolm said humbly, waiting to see if she caught what he said.

"Am I your queen?" Helen asked innocently.

Malcolm laughed, then said, "Yes ma'am. Don't you agree?"

"We shall see, Sir," replied Helen in a flirtatious voice.

"Hey, you can't knock a brother for exercising his faith. Talk with you soon, beautiful," Malcolm stated.

"I look forward to it," Helen said, laughing.

Joyful! Auntie Duty

After hanging up the phone, Helen received another call. It was Ashanti calling.

"Hey, Ashanti," Helen said as she answered the phone.

"Hey, Helen, what are you up to?"

"Nothing much," Helen answered. "I'm creating a marketing plan for my book. What are you up to?"

"Trying to find a babysitter so I can go to work. Can you watch the baby for me?" Ashanti asked.

"Sure. Bring me my princess!" Helen said happily.

"Well I don't have time to bring her to you, because I have to be at work in 30 minutes. Can you just come and pick her up?" Ashanti asked.

Irritated by the last-minute request, but joyful at the thought of spending time with her niece, Helen said, "Yeah, I will be on my way. What time will you be picking her up?"

Ashanti replied, "I get off work at 5:00 pm, so I will pick her up from your house at 6:00 pm. Thanks for watching her for me!" Ashanti answered with excitement.

"You're welcome. I'm on my way now." Helen said.

Helen hung up the phone, then went outside, got in her beautiful Mercedes Benz, and drove to her mother's house to pick up her niece.

While she was driving, Helen couldn't help but think about how annoying it was to have been called at the last minute for the tenth time in the past two months. Helen thought to herself, "I love my sister, but she is getting on my nerves with these last minute requests!"

After parking her car, Helen went up the snow-covered stairs, used her key to unlock her mother's door, then entered her home.

"Hey, Ma," Helen said, as she walked in the door. Inside, she saw her 55-year-old mother sitting on the couch reading the book "Hurt but Grateful" by Latresa Rice, and sat down beside her.

"Hey, honey, are you here to pick up your niece?" she asked.

"Yes, ma'am. Is she ready?"

"I don't know. Your sister is in the basement. Ask her," her mother said.

"Ok, Ma. How are you?" Helen inquired.

"I'm great, baby. Just glad you are picking her up so I can get some real rest," Mrs. Morris-Brown replied with a chuckle.

Helen laughed with her mother, then she yelled, "Ashanti!"

"We're coming, Sis! One sec," Ashanti called up.

Helen sat back down and continued to talk to her mother for about ten minutes. Then, Ashanti came up the stairs with Helen's niece and a purple, black, and gold-colored diaper bag that reeked of marijuana and musk.

"I miss you already, mommy's pretty baby," Ashanti said to her daughter. Then, she put a coat on the baby, placed her in her car seat, and handed it to Helen.

"We are about to have a blast!" Helen shouted with joy, as she looked at her niece. Then, she looked at Ashanti and uttered, "See you at 6:00 pm, Sis."

"I will be there, Sis. Thanks again for keeping her for me," Ashanti added.

"No problem, Sis," Helen assured her, as she left the house and placed the baby in the car seat securely in the back seat of the car.

While driving home, Helen played the song "How will I know" by Whitney Houston and was loudly singing along until she heard Tatiana screaming in the back seat.

Alarmed by the screams, she turned down her music and said, "What's wrong with Auntie's gorgeous baby? Don't cry, Pooh."

It appeared that her words were falling on deaf ears, because the screams kept getting louder and louder.

Helen pulled her car into an Obama gas station, quickly got out of the car, then went into the back seat to take the baby girl out of her car seat to rock her for a moment.

Rocking Tatiana was a fruitless effort. Helen searched the diaper bag for the baby's bottle. She found an almost empty bottle and a can of Enfamil with Iron that had less than one scoop of powder in it.

Helen returned the baby to her car seat, then gave her the almost empty bottle of milk. She propped it up using a blanket.

Instantly, the crying ceased. She took a deep breath and said, "Aww, Auntie's gorgeous baby is hungry. Auntie is going to get you some more milk, Pooh."

At that moment, Helen called her sister to let her know that there wasn't enough powder in the container to make the baby another bottle. While the phone was ringing, she thought to herself, "Tatiana is hungry right now and there isn't enough powder to make her another bottle of milk! Who sends a baby with someone and fails to make sure the baby has enough milk to drink? Ugh!"

Ashanti answered the phone saying, "Hey, Sis, what's wrong?"

Helen replied, "Hey, Sis. Tatiana was screaming because she was hungry, and you didn't put enough milk in the bag for me to make her another bottle. I am about to go back to Momma's house to get the milk. Where is it?"

"Sis, I actually don't have any more milk for her, because I don't have the money to buy it this week and Zadel doesn't have it either. Can you buy some for her and I will pay you back when I get my check? Please?"

Irritated at the inconvenience of this inconsiderate request, Helen looked back at her beautiful niece and said, "Yes, but I wish you would have told me that earlier. You need to ask me these things in advance, Sis. What if I didn't have enough money to buy her the milk she needs?"

Ashanti answered, saying, "Girl, bye, you always have it. Thanks so much, Sis! I love you!"

"Mmmmhmmm," Helen muttered, then ended the call. She pulled into the nearest CVS and parked her car three parking spots away from the door to the main entrance.

"Ok, Auntie's beautiful baby. Let's go get you some milk," Helen said to Tatiana in a cheerful, loving tone of voice, as she zipped up her three months size neon pink snow suit. Helen unbuckled her seat belt and placed a blanket over Tatiana's car seat to block the freezing cold air from her face.

Tatiana continued to drink her bottle while Helen called Ashanti to see if there was anything else the baby needed that she could purchase while she was at CVS. Since Ashanti did not answer the phone, Helen hung up, then carried the car seat with her niece in it into the CVS store.

After entering CVS and placing Tatiana in the shopping cart, she pushed her through the store looking for Enfamil with Iron. Frustrated because of her immediate need to purchase the formula before the baby's bottle ran out of milk, Helen turned to an employee that was standing in aisle two and asked, "Excuse me, Sir. Can you tell me which aisle I can locate Enfamil with Iron?"

Without even glancing up, the employee continued to stock the shelves and replied, "Aisle Four."

Helen pushed the shopping cart to aisle four, looking adoringly at her beautiful niece, smiling and singing to her as they went through the aisle. Tatiana took the bottle out of her mouth, giggled, and smiled back at Helen.

"Yes, here it is!" Helen exclaimed in excitement, as she grabbed the Enfamil with Iron and placed it in the shopping cart. Then, she pushed the cart to the front of the store to pay for it, while talking to Tatiana.

"Hi! I can help you in line one," a customer service representative said.

Helen quickly pushed Tatiana in the shopping cart over to line one. Upon approaching the counter, the cashier exclaimed, "Aww, she is so beautiful! What's your daughter's name?"

"She's not my daughter. She is my beautiful niece. Her name is Tatiana," Helen replied proudly.

After Helen mentioned Tatiana's name to the cashier, Tatiana started screaming at the top of her lungs. Her bottle was empty.

"It's ok, Auntie's beautiful baby. We are getting you some more milk right now, Pooh," Helen said to Tatiana, attempting to console her. "Aww, somebody is still hungry. Let me hurry and ring this up for you. Do you have a CVS card?" the cashier asked.

"Yes," replied Helen, passing the cashier her CVS card.

"Perfect, your total is $19.87," said the cashier.

"You must be kidding me! One container of this powdered milk cost $19.87 and nursing mothers produce this milk for their children for free? This little angel's mom needs to pump her milk and send it with her," Helen mumbled, irritated. After Helen paid for the Enfamil with Iron, she dressed Tatiana in all her outdoor winter accessories and pushed the baby in the cart to the car. Tatiana screamed when she put her in her car seat, and during the entire ride to Helen's home.

Helen pulled into the driveway, parked her car, and promptly took her beautiful niece into the house. "Hey, Auntie's baby! It's ok. Auntie has you. We are here, Pooh," Helen announced, as she bent her head down to kiss the baby's cheek.

Disturbed by the horrific odor that oozed from Tatiana's diaper, Helen quickly realized that she needed to change it, to set Tatiana free from the undesirable attachment to her own waste. Changing Tatiana's diaper also delivered Helen's nostrils from the violent assault they were experiencing, as the grotesque smell filled the air.

Helen wiped the defecation off the child's behind, gave her a soothing bath, then placed a new diaper on her buttock. Next, she swaddled her in a multicolored fleece blanket, then gave her a warm bottle and watched her slowly drift off to sleep.

"Yes, a sleeping baby! She Won!" Then, she decided to take a nap as well. After all, when a baby sleeps, it is in the babysitter's best interest to take a nap also, so that he or she can rest and be ready for the challenge of babysitting!

CHAPTER 3

Timekeepers

Startled by the sound of the "Thank You Haters" ringtone, as Latresa Rice's melodious voice sang an appreciation message to all haters who were calling, Helen jumped up and quickly answered the phone.

"Hello," she said.

"Hey, beautiful. Did I catch you at a bad time?" Malcolm asked.

"Any time you call me is always a great time," Helen replied, smiling. Blushing, Malcolm laughed and said, "Alright, pretty lady."

Helen responded with a chuckle. Immediately, Malcolm said, "I was calling because you were on my mind. I had a client cancel on me today and I was wondering if I could treat you to lunch."

"Awww, that is so sweet!" Helen exclaimed. "I can't right now, because I am preoccupied with caring for my beautiful niece. However, I can go out to dinner with you later if you like." She continued, "Does 7:00 pm work for you?"

"Listen, I will make it work. I need to see you again. It's a date!" "I mean yeah, that's cool," he quickly added, after he heard himself sounding a little too excited.

"Fantastic! See you at 7:00 pm," Helen stated.

"I will pick you up at your house at 7:00 pm. See you soon, my love," said Malcolm, then he promptly hung up the phone.

After ending her conversation with Malcolm, Helen called her sister to see what time she was picking up Tatiana.

"Hey, Ashanti, what time are you picking up Tatiana?" Helen asked. "I have a 7:00 pm appointment tonight, so I need you to pick her up by 6:00 pm."

"Hey, Sis! I can pick her up by 6:00. Thanks again for watching her for me. You're a lifesaver! Where's my baby now?" Ashanti asked.

"Auntie for the win!" Helen said, laughing out loud. "She is sound asleep. I changed her diaper, gave her a bath, a warm bottle of milk, a mini-back massage, and she has been sleep for the past three hours."

"What? I will try that next time, because home girl keeps me up and it seems like I barely ever get any rest," Ashanti responded with a hearty laugh.

"Ok, Sis, I am still at work, so I have to go; but I will see you in two hours." Helen said.

"No problem, Sis. Have a great time at work. See you soon," Ashanti retorted.

Helen hung up the phone. Since Helen was no longer sleepy, she decided to spend an hour writing her next book, while Tatiana slept peacefully. Then, she spent the remaining hour getting ready for her hot date.

"Yes, I am ready! She Cute!" Helen exclaimed, admiring herself in the mirror. "Let me see what time it is," she said.

Helen grabbed her phone and touched the screen. "It's 5:45," she exclaimed, then rushed to the window to see if Ashanti had arrived yet. She hadn't arrived. Anxiously waiting on Ashanti's arrival, Helen packed Tatiana's bag, then put the baby's snow suit on her. Suddenly, her doorbell rang. It was 6:00 pm sharp and Ashanti was at the door.

"Yes! Come on in. Thank you for being on time, Sis!" Helen exclaimed.

"No problem, Sis. Thanks for watching her for me," Ashanti stated.

Helen gave Tatiana to Ashanti. Immediately, Ashanti walked out of Helen's home toward her car, while carrying the baby in her car seat. Helen carried the baby's diaper bag and went outside as well. Then she opened Ashanti's car door and placed the diaper bag in the back seat.

"Bye, bye, Auntie's beautiful baby...dunt da dunt da dunt da dunt," Helen sang to Tatiana as Ashanti placed her in the car.

Tatiana flashed her aunt a beaming "million dollar" smile that warmed Helen's heart.

After Ashanti got into the driver's seat and closed the door, Helen waved goodbye to her sister, then went back into the house to finish preparing for her date. The eleven dates she experienced with Malcolm, after their first meeting at Star Chucks, were amazing! Helen always looked forward to their dates, and tomorrow night she was expecting another amazing experience.

Date Night

As usual, Helen's fine chocolate treat arrived on time to pick her up for their date.

When she noticed that he was outside, she put on her coat, exited her home, and walked toward the door on the passenger side of his truck. Then, she stood beside it patiently waiting for Malcolm to open it.

Malcolm got out of the truck, walked over to the passenger side door, and opened it, saying,

"Oooo weee! Girl, you are fine!" Helen smiled and said, "Thank you," then climbed onto the heated black and red leather seat in Malcolm's metallic black 2020 BMW truck.

"Where are we going, Sir?" Helen asked, gazing into Malcolm's eyes.

"It's a surprise, but I promise you will love it," Malcolm answered, as he buckled his seatbelt.

"Really? So, you think you know me, huh?" Helen replied with a chuckle.

"A real man pays attention to the woman he desires to share his life with," Malcolm said with a smile, as he winked at Helen and drove to their surprise dinner destination.

Once they arrived at Morton's Steakhouse, the valet attendant greeted Malcolm and Helen by name and gave Helen one red rose. Then, Malcolm took her by the hand and escorted her into the restaurant.

"Welcome," the hostess said warmly. "We have been expecting you, Mr. Peterson. Here's a rose for your lovely lady; feel free to take it from this vase. Now let me show you to your table," she said. "I hope you enjoy your dinner, Ms. Morris," she added with a joyful smile.

Malcolm thanked her and grabbed another long-stemmed red rose from the vase on the counter and presented it to Helen as they walked to their table. Helen was elated! She loved red roses; they have always been her favorite flower!" She thought to herself, "Alright, Malcolm! You are loving on me real heavy right now, but I made a promise to myself and God. I will remain celibate until marriage. Lord, help me! This brother is fine, and he smells like heaven stirred up its own special fragrance and placed it on him."

When they arrived at their table, Malcolm pulled out Helen's chair so she could be seated first, then he sat in his chair. The waiter approached their table. Before he asked them what they wanted to order, he placed a beautiful sky blue, gold, and chocolate-colored, sparkling vase on the table filled with water.

"Madam, may I take your flowers?" he asked Helen politely.

"Certainly," she replied, passing her two flowers to the waiter.

While Helen was talking to Malcolm, the waiter cut the stems of the flowers in a slant, then placed them in the water. He also placed an additional rose in the vase located in the center of the table. As Helen gazed at the beautiful vase, she noticed that her two flowers had increased. There were now three roses in the vase.

"Hmmm, I wonder what this man is up to?" Helen pondered, until her thoughts were interrupted by the waiter's question.

"Are you both ready to order? Ladies first, of course."

"Helen, what would you like?" Malcolm asked.

"I would like to order the T-bone steak well-done, loaded mashed potatoes, steamed broccoli, a Caesar side salad, and an apple martini," Helen replied.

Malcolm smiled and said, "I'll have what she is having, plus a side of the market lobster and a glass of Merlot."

"Excellent choice!" exclaimed the waiter, as he waved for someone to bring a tray with various uncooked steaks and lobster. He described the different cuts of meat, then asked Malcolm and Helen to choose which steaks and lobster they wanted the chef to cook.

After they made their selections, the waiter's new trainee passed another red rose to the waiter. Then, the waiter cut the rose and placed it in the vase.

Malcolm and Helen continued to talk, as the waiter brought their side Caesar salads, fresh rolls, and drinks to the table. Before he left the table, he brought out another red rose, cut off the end, and added it to Helen's vase. Malcolm held Helen's hand, as he blessed the food through prayer. After the prayer, Helen couldn't take the suspense any longer.

"Malcolm, what is the story behind these gorgeous roses?" Helen asked, deeply inhaling their rich fragrance.

Malcolm smiled mysteriously and said, "I will tell you after dinner, my love."

As soon as they finished their salads, their dinner arrived. The food smelled and looked scrumptious!

The waiter brought another red rose to the table, cut the stem, placed it in Helen's vase and said, "Enjoy your meal."

They ate and laughed hysterically. The waiter returned to their table and gave Malcolm a bouquet of six red roses with the stems already trimmed.

"Would you like to have dessert?" he asked politely.

"Yes, I will have the New York style cheesecake," Helen stated, smiling. Malcolm slid the waiter a $200 tip, looked into Helen's eyes then he lowered his voice and said, "I'm looking at my dessert, but I will wait another six months, if she will have me."

The waiter smiled at Helen before leaving the table. Malcolm then turned to her and said, "Helen, I know we have only been dating for six months, but I feel like I've known you my whole life and I can't imagine going through life without you."

Suddenly, Malcolm got out of his seat, went over to Helen's chair, kneeled in front of her, and pulled out a 2-carat, princess cut diamond ring with a white gold band from his left pants pocket. He passed her the most recent bouquet of flowers and said, "Will you allow me the pleasure of courting you for the next six months as my fiancée?" At that moment, Helen realized that the first six red roses represented the six months of dating, and the bouquet of six red roses represented Malcolm's desire to court her for the next six months before marrying her!

With tears in her eyes, Helen shouted, with a resounding, "Yes!" and the entire restaurant erupted in applause. Malcolm smiled and kissed her passionately. Then, Helen put the remaining six roses in the vase and shared her cheesecake with Malcolm, as they continued to enjoy their time in the restaurant. When they finished their meal, Malcolm paid the bill, then helped Helen put on her coat.

Helen assumed that the gorgeous vase was supposed to be left at the restaurant so she asked, "Malcolm, is someone coming back to wrap up my flowers so that I can take them with me?"

"Baby, I had this vase specially made for you, using all of your favorite colors. They can stay in the vase because we are taking it with us," Malcolm said tenderly.

A tear rolled down Helen's cheek as she thought to herself, "God is so faithful! He never stopped listening to me. Thank you, Lord, for blessing me with the desires of my heart at the appropriate time. I'm ready."

"Baby, are you ok?" Malcolm asked in a concerned tone of voice.

Helen replied, "I'm fine, honey. No one has ever done anything like this for me and I feel so special. Thank you," she said, then leaned in to kiss him.

At that moment, Malcolm grabbed her face with both hands and said to her, "That day is over. I am going to love you to such an extent that you will forget any pain you ever experienced. You are worth it. I love you, Helen," then he kissed her passionately until the valet driver pulled up with his vehicle.

The driver opened the door for Helen, and Malcolm gave him a $30 tip. Then, he drove Helen home, walked with her to the front door, and kissed her good night.

Over the next three months, Ashanti continued to call Helen at the last minute for various things, ranging from keeping Tatiana over the weekend, to borrowing money for diapers.

Whenever Helen would mention how these things made her feel, Ashanti would get an attitude and say, "Nobody wants to help me, but that's cool. Me and my baby are going to be justfine! You don't have to do nothing for her. I guess she will just be hungry, since I can't produce the milk, her daddy doesn't have any money, and her auntie just won't get her any food to eat."

Helen also noticed that, unlike her first time babysitting Tatiana, every other time she watched her, Ashanti was 30 minutes up to 2 hours late picking her up. She also would have an excuse as to why she could not pick her up on time. Each time she was late, Helen had to reschedule her appointments or cancel them. This vicious cycle caused the excited, "eager to help" aunt to become the "upset, unavailable to help" aunt. Helen decided to brace herself, just in case she experienced the same type of behaviors from Ariel this weekend when she would be babysitting Shawn.

New Outlook on Babysitting

At noon on May 18, 2020, Ariel called Helen to confirm that she would still be able to watch Shawn for her that Friday, May 22nd at 6:00 pm, through Sunday, May 24th.

Helen was impressed with Ariel's follow up call. It seemed like Ariel was so thoughtful and organized. Helen returned Ariel's call and confirmed that she would watch Shawn for Ariel. Over the next four days, Helen spent time with her fiancé and finished writing her second book, titled "Living Diamonds." Finally, it was Friday and Helen was excited to greet Ariel at the door. She arrived promptly at 6:00 pm.

"Hey, beautiful! It feels like it's been centuries since I've seen you. How have you been?" Ariel asked, carrying Shawn into Helen's home.

"I've been fantastic! I finished writing my book and now I am engaged to the love of my life! How are you?" Helen inquired.

"Girl, that is awesome! Oh, my goodness! I didn't know! Congrats! I love to hear good news!" Ariel exclaimed. "Well, I have to hurry up and leave so that I can get on the plane in time. Here's Shawn's bottle. He has three additional bottles in his diaper bag. Also, this stuffed Buzz Lightyear is his favorite toy, so I'm going to leave it with you. I prepared a milk bottle for him to drink when he wakes up. If you have any issues, please call me. Thank you again for helping me. I appreciate you," replied Ariel. Then she smiled and hugged Helen.

"Girl, it's not a problem. That's what family is for. He is so handsome! Go enjoy yourself!"

"Love you!" Helen exclaimed, rushing Ariel out the door so she would not be late for her flight.

After she closed the door, she quickly picked up the sleeping five-month-old baby boy from his car seat to take his coat off. Shawn was a handsome, chocolate baby boy with dimples and dark curly hair. He smelled like Dove gentle soap, lavender baby lotion, and baby powder. Shawn weighed approximately 18 lbs. As Helen unzipped his coat, he woke up, startled, and immediately started crying loudly.

"Aww, don't cry, young king. It's ok. Are you hungry?" Helen asked him, holding him, as she warmed up his milk bottle. Shawn continued to scream and cry. In response, Helen made up this song and sang it to him:

"You are a handsome king.

You reign over yourself.

You reign above finances.

Nothing can stop your progress.

You will walk in your dreams. And live abundantly.

Shawn, you are a blessing; keep being who you are."

Immediately the baby stopped crying and smiled at her. However, when Shawn saw Helen take the bottle out of the water, tears flowed from his eyes. Then, glass-shattering screams were heard again.

She consoled the baby, as she checked the temperature of the milk by putting several drops of it on the inside of her wrist. It was not too hot!

Helen promptly gave the baby his bottle, as she held him and continued to sing the song that she affectionately named, "Shawn's Theme Song" to him. Once he finished his bottle, he babbled happily to Helen. She responded to him, as if she fully understood what he was saying, while burping him. Then, he burped twice and fell asleep. Helen rose from her leather reclining chair to lay him down.

After she laid Shawn on his back in the baby crib that she kept at home for her niece, she tiptoed out of the room and went into her home office to write. For Helen, writing was life! She was so excited to be able to write her next book. The baby slept for about three hours. During that time, Helen was able to wash clothes, write six pages of her upcoming book, and talk to her fiancé.

Curious about what Ariel may have sent with Shawn, Helen checked Shawn's diaper bag. Inside were the following items:

- nine changes of clothes

- six pairs of pajamas

- three bottles

- one can of Enfamil with Iron

- a Nose Frida thermometer

- Johnson's lavender baby lotion

- Johnson's baby powder with corn starch

- Johnson's baby oil

- three fleece blankets

- eight bibs

- two teething rings

- a bag of size three diapers

Helen answered with a resounding

There was also a baby brush and comb set, a selection of Plum Organics baby food, several jars of Gerber baby food, some Gerber cereal, a rattle, six pairs of socks, three pairs of baby shoes, six baby wash cloths, a Veggie Tales DVD, an A-B-C DVD, a counting DVD, a white envelope with Helen's name on it, and a first-aid kit.

"Wow! Ariel packed everything in the bag except the kitchen sink!" exclaimed Helen, impressed by all the details.

"I wonder what's in the envelope?" Helen pondered, as she opened it. Ariel's letter read:

Dear Helen,

I can't thank you enough for keeping Shawn for me. I appreciate your sacrifice. Although you didn't ask me for anything, as a token of my appreciation for watching my son, I have enclosed $25. I wish I could give you more; but this is the best I can do right now. I love you and, once again, thank you."

As she read Ariel's letter, tears flowed down Helen's cheeks. Helen thought about the fact that, out of all the children that she had watched, no one had ever written her an appreciation letter, given her any money to keep their child, or simply made sure that their child had everything they might need while the parent was away. With a huge smile on her face, Helen exclaimed, "It is a great feeling to know that the people you love and sacrifice for actually appreciate you!"

CHAPTER 4

Access Granted

Helen placed the letter in the "essential mail" container in her office, took a shower, oiled her walnut-colored skin and put on her pajamas. She ensured that Shawn was still sleeping peacefully, then she went to sleep.

At 8:00 am Saturday morning, this beautiful "human alarm clock" screamed to such an extent that Helen was startled awake. She quickly reached into the crib to pick up Shawn, then checked his diaper to see if the scream was due to him feeling as if his gluteus-maximus was soaking in a sagging sponge. As she suspected, his diaper was soaking wet. Helen promptly gave Shawn a bath, dried him off, put baby powder on his pro-creation tool, and wrapped it up in a crisp, white Huggies diaper.

As she looked into his adorable eyes, while he was cooing at her, she smiled, gave him a warm milk bottle, held him close to her heart, then turned on the TV to watch "The Incredibles 2" movie.

While only half-watching the movie, Helen reflected on her experience babysitting Shawn so far. Despite being awakened by Shawn's screams, he was such a sweet baby, but at least he slept peacefully through the night. Over the remaining two days, Helen had a blast enjoying her time with Shawn.

Whenever Shawn was sleep during the day, she would use that time to speak with her fiancé or work on her book.

However, Sunday at 1:00 pm, Malcolm called Helen with an unusual request. His request heightened her desire to marry him.

Malcolm said, "Hey baby, you've been working so hard on your book while you've been watching Shawn, I know you need a moment to rest. Is it ok if I come over to your house, run you some bath water, tend to Shawn, and cook you a scrumptious meal while you relax in the tub?"

Helen's eyes widened to the size of golf balls in amazement at the request. She could not believe what she was hearing. Here's a fine man who desired to cook for her and take care of Shawn so that she could indulge in self-care with no strings attached…WOW! Immediately, Helen replied, "Oooooweee, man I love you! Thank you, honey. I don't mind at all. What time are you coming?"

"Depends on what type of meal my angel desires tonight. What would you like to eat for dinner, beautiful?" Malcolm inquired.

"I would love to eat steak, lobster, and shrimp alfredo with steamed broccoli," Helen replied.

"Oh ok," he laughed. "It's going to take me some time to prepare that type of meal, but what my lady wants, she gets. I'll be there at 2:00 pm," Malcolm stated, still chuckling.

"Can't wait to watch you cook this meal, my love. You

are simply amazing!”

“I’m just a man in love with a woman that I believe is more precious than anything one can desire on earth. I plan to spend the rest of my life making sure that she feels my love for her. I love you,” he said in a soft voice.

“I love you, too. See you soon, my king,” Helen said, excited at the thought of an afternoon and evening of pampering. Then, she blew a kiss to Malcolm into the phone, and he sent an air kiss back to her.

After this exchange, she hung up the phone and immediately thought to herself, “Wait! Should I go put my clothes on, do my hair, etc. now, or wait for him to get here? He has never been at my house without me being dressed up and looking cute. What would he think of me if he knew that I was just sitting here in my pajamas tending to this handsome baby?”

As a host of thoughts bombarded her mind, Helen finally decided that she wouldn’t worry about it. She said to herself, “He is going to have to see me dressed down one day anyway. I guess today is the day, because it doesn’t make sense to change my clothes if he is going to run me some bath water. I will just wait for Malcolm to get here.”

Helen leaned back in her seat and continued to cuddle Shawn, marveling at how attentive he was to the movie.

At exactly 2:00 pm, Helen's doorbell rang. She placed Shawn in his car seat and went to open the door for Malcolm.

"Hello, handsome, you are always on time," Helen said with a smile.

Standing at the front door with a look of adoration on his face, as he gazed into her eyes, Malcolm said, "I'm actually late, because I tried to be here by 1:45 pm, since the opportunity to look at my fine lady is always worth it. Now, let me in, Boo." Helen blushed as she unlocked the door and let her fiancé into the house.

"I can't believe that he said nothing about me still being in pajamas. He still believes that I am beautiful, even with my hair all over my head and I'm dressed in these run-down pajamas! Yes, he is stuck with me!" Helen thought to herself.

As Malcolm entered her home, he immediately noticed the baby sleeping in his car seat. He quickly placed the groceries for the exquisite meal for two in the kitchen, then went into her private bathroom to prepare the bath for Helen, as promised.

Helen, on the other hand, sat on her couch next to the baby and continued to watch TV, while he rested. Suddenly, her focus came to a halt, hearing the words, "Baby, your luxurious bath awaits your presence. I've got Shawn. See you in around

30 minutes."

Excited and eager to see what Malcolm had done, Helen quickly arose from the couch and walked towards the bathroom. To her surprise, red rose petals showered the path from the living room to the bathroom.

When she entered the bathroom, she was greeted with the smell of lavender, and a gorgeous cluster of white bubbles that looked like clouds dancing on the rose petal-sprinkled bath water.

"Awwww I feel so special! Thank you, honey," Helen said with excitement.

"You are welcome baby, see you soon," Malcolm replied with a smile. Then, he picked up the baby's car seat and carried Shawn closer to the kitchen; so he could keep an eye on the baby while he prepared a delicious meal for them to enjoy.

While relaxing in the tub, Helen thought to herself, "This food is smelling good! I have a man that can cook! Wait a minute. I also haven't heard Shawn cry. This man is good with children too? WOW! Where has he been my whole life! I can't wait to get out of this tub and enjoy a meal with my king. Just call me, Blessed and Highly favored."

After taking her relaxing bath and getting dressed, she brushed her teeth, did her make up, and fixed her hair. Then, she emerged from the bathroom like a radiant royal queen, presenting herself before her king.

"You look absolutely gorgeous, baby," Malcolm said, staring at her as if she was the most beautiful work of art that he had ever seen.

"Thank you, honey!" Helen replied, blushing as she lifted Shawn from his car seat. While she was holding Shawn, Helen noticed that Malcolm had set the dining room table with 14 kt gold- trimmed glassware, gold silverware, and white plates with gold edging that he had brought with him. She was amazed at how much effort he put into this moment. As one tear rolled down her left cheek, she heard Malcolm ask the following question:

"Are you ready to eat baby, because dinner is served," Malcolm announced.

"I already fed the baby and changed him. As you can see, your man has some skills," Malcolm said, laughing.

"I see," replied Helen, looking at Malcolm with admiration.

Ding Dong

"That's the doorbell, honey," Helen called to Malcolm. "I think that's Ariel. Can you help me make sure that all of Shawn's things are in his bag?" she asked.

"Absolutely, baby," replied Malcolm, as he thought to himself, "Yes! Now, I will be able to spend some alone time with my boo! Let me hurry up and make sure that this young prince's things are packed." Malcolm promptly went to the bedroom in the back of the house to search for any items that belonged to the baby.

As Helen held Shawn, she got up from the table and went to answer the front door.

"Who is it?" Helen asked.

"It's me, Ariel," a voice answered.

Helen immediately opened the door. "Hey girl! Come on in!" she exclaimed, welcoming her inside.

Ariel reached for her son. The handsome chocolate baby boy smiled at his mother and reached for her in response, then Helen gave Shawn to Ariel.

"Hi, mommy's handsome prince! I missed you!" Ariel said to Shawn, kissing him on both cheeks.

The baby kept laughing and smiling during this interaction with his mother. Helen's face beamed, as she watched how Ariel lovingly embraced her baby. Immediately, Helen's observation was interrupted with a question.

"It smells so good in here! What are you cooking, girl, and can we have a plate?" Ariel joked. At that moment, Malcolm came out of the bedroom with more of Shawn's toys.

"That lovely smell is courtesy of Helen's chef and soon-to-be husband," her fiancéanswered.

Then, he extended his right hand towards Ariel and said, "My name is Malcolm. You must be Ariel."

Ariel was shocked! With one hand holding Shawn and the other one free, she smiled, then extended her free hand to shake Malcolm's.

"Well…well…well, it's nice to meet you, Malcolm. I am certain that I will be seeing you around more often," Ariel said, smiling and winking at Helen.

"Let's get out of here so the two of you can enjoy your delicious meal. Helen, I can't thank you enough for watching Shawn for me. I appreciate everything that you do for us."

"It's not a problem. He is such a good baby!" Helen added, walking Ariel and Shawn to the door.

Malcolm assisted Ariel by carrying Shawn's car seat and diaper bag to the car.

Ariel thanked Malcolm for his help, promptly secured her baby into his seat, then got in her car and drove away.

Helen looked at the clock. She noticed that Ariel had arrived 15 minutes earlier than the time she said she would be arriving to pick up her son. At that moment, she thought to herself, "I love it when people respect my time. I would definitely watch Shawn again in the future."

Then, Malcolm came back inside the home. The two of them enjoyed their delicious meal while watching a movie and laughing hysterically, until it was time for Malcolm to go home.

Duty Calls

"The early bird gets the worm," Helen said aloud, as she forced herself to rise from her bed at 5:00 am.Awake, but still sleepy, Helen pressed play to listen to an audio recorded daily devotional while she was enroute to the shower. This cyclical process was a necessary part of her preparation ritual before writing her books.

After embracing the rock salt-like droplets of water that rained down on her during her shower, she dried herself off and put on her favorite powder blue jogging suit.

"Finally, a day off from work! Yes!" Helen thought to herself, as she sat down to write three pages of her book. "I should go to Belle Isle and sit by the water," she pondered. Helen was lost in a web of joyful thoughts, until they were interrupted by the sound of her phone ringing.

"Hello, this is Helen," she answered.

"Hey, Sis, how are you?" Ashanti asked.

"I'm good, Sis," Helen replied while thinking to herself, "I wish she would just get to the point of her call. She never just calls me to check on me. There is always an ulterior motive."

"That's good. I need a favor," Ashanti said. "Can you watch your niece for just two hours? I promise that I will pick her up by 3:00 pm. I really need to go to the doctor because I feel sick. I know that they will not allow me to take her with me."

Helen hesitated to respond, as she reflected on her babysitting efforts for her sister over the past two years. Although in the very beginning she used to arrive on time to pick up Tatiana, over the past two years she was late picking her up. Sometimes Helen caught Ashanti in a lie when she explained why she needed Helen to babysit. Often, Ashanti failed to send money, clothing, food, and other essentials with Tatiana, and became argumentative with Helen when she attempted to discuss these issues with her. Helen loves her niece, but she felt unappreciated and used.

Finally, Helen decided to respond to Ashanti.

"Sis, you know I love you and my niece, but I did have other plans for the day. Is Zadel able to watch Tatiana for you today?"

"I asked him already, but he said he has to work. Can you watch her for me, please? I know I was two hours late last time. I promise that I will be on time this time. I just really need you to do this favor for me, Sis. Please," she implored.

"Ok, but only for two hours. Make sure you are on time," Helen responded, irritated.

"I said I would be there on time. Dang, you don't have to tell me what to do all the time. Thanks again for watching her. We will be there in 15 minutes. Love you, Sis."

"Love you, too," Helen responded, then she pressed her lips together like two opposing magnets, as she did her best to avoid cursing Ashanti out for making that snippy remark.

"I am sick of being my sister's keeper! She'd better be here on time," Helen muttered to herself, gazing down at her gym shoes, mentally readjusting her plans to assist her sister in extinguishing her emergency situation: the need for a babysitter.

She took three deep breaths, then continued to write her

next best seller. Within 15 minutes, Ashanti and her friend Jerica arrived with Tatiana. She grabbed her baby girl out of her car seat, put the handle of the diaper bag on her left shoulder, walked up the porch stairs, and knocked on the front door.

"Who is it?" Helen asked.

"It's me, Sis," replied Ashanti.

Immediately, Helen opened the door. When the toddler saw her Aunt Helen, she smiled at her and raised her arms in an "I surrender" position, as a formal request to be picked up. With great joy, Helen returned the endearing smile, then embraced her niece.

"Here's her bag. I put some snacks, extra Pull-Ups, her favorite juice, a change of clothes,wipes, and some other things in it that she might need.

"Thanks again for helping me, Sis," Ashanti said to Helen, as she passed her the diaper bag.

Helen was shocked as she looked at all the supplies Ashanti had brought for the baby.

Helen smiled at her sister, picked up the diaper bag, and said, "Thank you. See you in two hours, Sis."

At that moment, Ashanti left the house to go to the car. As she watched her sister walk to the car, Helen noticed that

Jerica was sitting in the passenger seat.

"Why is she with her? Every time she is with Jerica, they get into some mess, then I have to bail them out. She'd better be going to the doctor and return here in two hours," Helen thought to herself, as she closed the door and shifted her focus to spending quality time with her niece.

Doctor Visit

"Thanks for going with me to the doctor, girl," Ashanti said to Jerica.

"No problem. You know I have your back, right?" Jerica replied.

"Yes, girl. I can't wait to find out what's going on with me," Ashanti said.

"Ashanti Morris," announced the nursing assistant.

Immediately, Ashanti arose from her seat and followed the nurse through the door to get examined by the doctor.

"Hi, Miss Morris, can you tell me what brings you in today?" the doctor asked.

"I have a burning sensation when I urinate. I need to know if I have an STD?" Ashanti asked, looking worried.

"Have you had unprotected sex recently?"

"Yes," Ashanti admitted.

"Ok. With your permission, we will run some tests to see if you have contracted a sexually transmitted disease," the doctor told her.

After Ashanti signed the release and "Permission To Provide Care" paperwork, the doctor ran several tests, then came back into the hospital room where Ashanti was and reported the findings.

"Miss Morris, our lab results indicate that you do not have Chlamydia, Gonorrhea, or any other STD that may cause a burning sensation. However, you do have a urinary tract infection. I will provide you with a prescription to fill. You are free to go. Have a great day, Miss Morris."

With great joy, Ashanti replied, "Thank you!" then gathered her things and left the hospital with Jerica.

After getting into the car, Ashanti said to Jerica, "Girl, I thought Zay had cheated on me again and gave me an STD. I was certain he did, so I punched holes in all his tires while his car was in the parking lot at his job. I feel so bad! The doctor said that I have a urinary tract infection. What should I do?" Ashanti asked her friend.

"You did what? That's my girl! That was some straight thug life stuff, girl! But for real, I don't know. You can't tell him that you did that. Wait until he calls you and then offer to pick him up," Jerica suggested.

"You're right. Girl, I feel terrible! What time is it?" Ashanti asked.

"10 minutes to 3:00 pm," replied Jerica.

"Oh no! Helen is going to be so mad if I don't get there within the next 10 minutes," Ashanti exclaimed, as she sped out of the hospital parking lot toward Helen's house.

After arriving at Helen's house, Ashanti jumped out of the car, ran to the front door, and knocked on it.

"Who is it?" Helen inquired.

"It's me, Sis" replied Ashanti.

Helen rolled her eyes while holding Tatiana, then opened the door. "Two hours, huh?" Helen said sarcastically.

"It's really not my fault this time. I went to the doctor, and it took me longer to be seen than I expected," replied Ashanti.

"I bet it did. This is really messed up. Every time you

need me, I am here to help you, but you don't seem to care about anything that I have to do. You probably didn't even go to the doctor," Helen retorted.

"I DID GO! I don't have to prove nothing to you. Give me my baby and we will be out."

"You make me sick! Always thinking someone is lying to you. I admit that I did lie to you a few times, but this time I'm not lying. You want to see my discharge paperwork from the hospital? I didn't mean to be 20 minutes late. I got stopped by a train on my way over here from the doctor. Look at my paperwork for yourself. Dang!" Ashanti exclaimed.

Helen noticed that today's date was on the paper that Ashanti waved in front of her to review, but she was still angry. Yet again, Ashanti was late picking up her child. Helen replied with an attitude, "I don't want to look at it. That's your business. You are just going to have to find someone else to watch her from this day forward, because I am done! You never do what you say you are going to do, and it always puts me in a bad position. I am sick of this!" Helen shouted at Ashanti.

Ashanti grabbed Tatiana and her belongings, placed her in the car seat and angrily drove away. Then, Helen left the house, locked her front door, and drove to a nearby park to relax and clear her mind of the drama she had just experienced.

Frustrated and annoyed with her sister, Ashanti arrived home, placed Tatiana in her crib with a warm bottle of milk, and then called Zadel.

"Hey babe, I'm almost finished with work. What's up?" Zadel whispered, as he answered his cell phone in the restroom at his job.

"I was calling to tell you about my results from the STD test that I took at the hospital," Ashanti explained.

"Ok. If you have an STD, it's because you have been cheating on me. Like I told you, I don't cheat on you anymore. I promised that I would stop because I wanted us to be a family. You keep holding me to my past, man. This is ridiculous! So, what did the doctor say?" he asked.

"Well, if you really haven't been cheating, you wouldn't be nervous about what the doctor said. Anyway, it's your lucky day because I don't have an STD. I have a urinary tract infection," Ashanti told Zadel.

"Yeah, ok, man. Whatever. Baby, I will be there in a few minutes, once I punch out,"

Zadel said.

"Oh, ok," replied Ashanti, then hung up the phone.

"Oh my goodness! What am I going to say when he calls me back about his tires?" Ashanti thought, panicking.

Five minutes later, her phone rang. It was Zadel. He sounded furious, saying, "Somebody slashed all four of my tires, so I'm stuck at work! I don't know who would have done this. It seems like every time I try to do right, something bad happens to me," Zadel groaned. "I'm about to call a tow truck to tow my car to our house. Can you come pick me up, baby?" he asked.

"Oh my goodness! That's terrible! I'm sorry that happened to you, honey," Ashanti replied, trying to sound upset and sympathetic. "Of course, I can come and pick you up. Let me get Tatiana ready and we will be on our way."

"Ok baby, see you soon," Zadel calmly replied.

"Yes! He didn't suspect that it was me! I am so glad," Ashanti thought to herself, feeling relieved. "I will make sure that I do better next time. I have to control my anger. I don't want to lose him. We have been through so much and he really has been trying to change. I feel terrible!" Ashanti thought to herself as ended the call."

Gathering the sleeping toddler, Ashanti put on her coat and shoes, then got into the vehicle and drove to pick up Zadel.

"Hey, baby," Ashanti said, as she arrived to pick up Zadel.

Acting nonchalant, Zadel got into the car, then turned to look her in the eyes."I know you are the one who cut my tires," he said confronting Ashanti. "What I don't know is, why? And don't lie to me, because we replayed the video footage from the parking lot. Why did you do that?" he implored, sounding hurt.

With tears flowing like a waterfall, Ashanti cried, "I'm sorry! I was angry because I thought you had cheated on me again and gave me an STD. I did it before I went to the doctor. I am so sorry! It won't happen again. I am trying to trust you. I'm so sorry. Please forgive me. I will pay to get them all fixed," she quickly added.

"I'm not even mad anymore. I'm disappointed. After all that I have been doing to show you that I'm not the same dude you met before our baby was born, you turn around and do this to me? I can fix my own tires. If you do something like this again though, we are done. Do you understand me?" Zadel said sharply.

"Yes baby. I'm sorry!" Ashanti said, sobbing. Zadel embraced her, then sat back in the passenger seat. After Zadel put on his seatbelt, Ashanti drove them home while Tatiana continued to sleep in her car seat.

Chapter 5

Appearances

"Yes! It's Friday and I can't wait to spend time with my honey all weekend! Malcolm is the best gift that God has blessed me with," Helen thought to herself, as she sat in her leather office chair, meditating on how much she needed a vacation.

"This weekend, Malcolm is taking me someplace special. I wonder where he could be taking me?" Helen pondered. "Maybe he is planning to take me to that new restaurant downtown. Or maybe he is planning to take me sky diving," Helen fantasized while sitting in her chair, until her thoughts were interrupted by the sound of the telephone ringing. She looked over her shoulder at the phone that was sitting on the left side of her desk, as if the caller had a contagious disease that would leap off the screen into her system. "Oh, it's just Ariel," Helen sighed as she answered the phone.

"Hey, girl! How are you?" Helen asked.

"Hey! I am good. How are you?" Ariel answered.

"I'm fantastic! I can't wait to get things together so that I can enjoy this weekend with my love," Helen exclaimed.

"Y'all are too cute! I am so happy for you. I can't wait to attend the wedding!" Ariel joyfully shouted.

"Yes! I am looking forward to it," Helen said. "I know you didn't call me just to talk about Malcolm. What's up?"

Laughing, Ariel replied, "You are right. I need a favor. Can you watch Shawn for me for three hours tonight? I know it's last minute and I am so sorry for even asking you this late. My supervisor called me 15 minutes ago, saying that he had to take an emergency flight to check on his mother who was admitted to the hospital and he can't cancel the meeting he has scheduled with a client. He wants me to meet with the client. I can give you $100 for the inconvenience.Can you help me?" Ariel pleaded.

"Tonight? Of course. Girl, had you said tomorrow, I would have said no. Now bring me my baby," Helen said, laughing.

"I love you! You are a lifesaver! I will call my supervisor now and tell him that I will be able to meet with the client, then I will bring Shawn to you at 5:00 pm. Is that a good time for you?" Ariel asked.

"Yes, ma'am," Helen replied.

"Ok, see you then!" Ariel said, sounding relieved.

Ariel arrived promptly at 5:00 with Shawn. He was well-dressed, smelling like lavender baby lotion and powder. Helen embraced the toddler with joy.

"I have to hurry up to get to my meeting, but I placed the $100 in his diaper bag. Thanks again!" Ariel exclaimed.

"No problem. I need his car seat, because we are going shopping," Helen requested.

Ariel went to the car, grabbed Shawn's car seat, and gave it to Helen. They hugged one another, then Ariel returned to her car and drove to her appointment.

When Helen opened the diaper bag, she saw that all of Shawn's necessities were inside, and there was a note that listed the time he ate his last meal before arriving, his allergies, and an emergency contact, in case she doesn't answer her phone. Helen secured the toddler's car seat in her car, placed him in it, and drove to the mall.

While they were in the mall, Helen allowed Shawn to play in the play area, then she took him to Olga's to eat some Snackers pita chips and fries. After Helen had finished her shopping, they returned to her house. Shawn was still asleep in his car seat when Ariel arrived promptly at 7:00 pm to pick him up. Helen had such a great time with Shawn that she took a host of pictures of their interactions and texted some of them to Ariel.

Shortly after Ariel picked him up, Ashanti called. Helen hesitated to answer the call, but she decided to do so.

"Hey, Sis, how are you?" Helen asked.

"I'm good. How are you? Ashanti replied.

"I'm good. What's up?" Helen questioned.

"Well, I wanted to say that I was sorry for having an attitude the last time you watched Tatiana for me. I was just angry because I felt like you never want to help me anymore, and when you do help me by watching my baby, you get an attitude with me for little petty stuff. I don't mean to always ask you to watch her for me, but I don't have anybody else," Ashanti explained.

"Momma said she is not going to watch her anymore, Zadel always has to work, and nobody else is willing to watch her. It's ridiculous that I can't even depend on family to help me in my time of need. We are supposed to have each other's back." Ashanti went on.

"I just don't understand why nobody wants to watch my baby or help me out anymore. I get angry when you act like you don't want to do it, because you are my older sister. As her aunt, you should be the first person that is always willing to watch her for me. At least, that's how I feel about it. But I'm sorry for yelling," she said apologetically.

"Is she serious? This is the worst apology she could have given, but this is a step in the positive direction, so I'll take it," Helen thought to herself, then she responded to Ashanti by saying, "I accept your apology. I love you and Tatiana, so of course I want to help you with her, Ashanti, but there is a difference between helping and enabling. There is helping someone, and there is feeling used by them," Helen commented. "I feel like many times you don't appreciate what I do for you or Tatiana. I feel like you often completely disrespect me by not considering my time and taking me for granted."

Helen continued. "For example, you send Tatiana over to my house without a diaper bag, and her clothes may be dirty, or she may not have a change of clothes at all. So, I must go buy outfits for her to keep at my house, then I don't have any money to cover any additional food expenses, or take her somewhere fun, etc. Tatiana is not the reason why people don't want to watch her. It's your behavior that causes people to refuse to help you. When you don't pick up your child on time, it causes me to be behind on the things that I planned to accomplish with the 24 hours that God has given me to live. You can't live my life and yours, too," Helen stated firmly.

"I saw your paperwork, so I know you were telling the truth about going to the doctor this time. I'm willing to start over with helping you, but you have to help yourself. You need to start making changes regarding how you treat those who are assisting you by watching your child. Tatiana is your responsibility. You chose to bring this beautiful baby into this world. It is not our responsibility to always be available to care for her. An entitlement mentality always causes great hardship for the one who possesses it. I love you. Let's start over," Helen concluded.

Ashanti was in tears. While Helen was speaking, at moments, Ashanti was joyful, and at other moments, she was angry. She didn't feel like she had taken advantage of anyone and felt like they should be willing to do more to help her. But she didn't want to argue with her sister anymore, so she decided to simply say, "I love you too, Sis. I want to start over as well."

Helen and Ashanti stayed on the phone for an hour, laughing and talking about the new words that Tatiana had learned, until Helen received a call from Malcolm.

"Sis, I have to call you back," Helen said, as her other phone line was ringing.

"Ok, Sis, I'm glad we worked things out. Love you. Talk to you tomorrow."

"I love you, too," Helen replied, then ended the call with Ashanti and answered Malcolm's call.

"Hey, my love," Helen said into the phone.

"Hey, honey, I was wondering, did you buy your wedding dress yet?" Malcolm asked.

"Yes. Why are you asking?" Helen asked, in a curious

tone of voice.

"Because, I want you to bring it with you this weekend. I got us two tickets to Las Vegas. I can't imagine spending another night without you in my arms as my wife. Let's get married this weekend," Malcolm asked, excitedly.

Helen was shocked and elated. She quickly answered, "Yes sir! What time will you be picking me up, because I need to pack?"

"Just pack your essentials and bring your bridal gown. Clothes, shoes, and any other items you need, I'll buy for you when we get there. See you at 12:00 noon tomorrow, my gorgeous bride to be."

ABOUT THE AUTHOR

"When life gives you lemons, you have what you need to make a delectable lemon dessert."- Latresa Rice

The above statement exemplifies the life of Latresa Rice. When she was seven years old, her mother died of AIDS. She lost her father in 2011, due to complications compounded by HIV. In 2020, her grandmother died and, one month later, her husband died from COVID-19 after only five months of marriage. Despite dealing with the various transitions of her loved ones, Ms. Rice has been able to accomplish a plethora of things.

In 2004, she graduated from the University of Michigan-Dearborn with a dual bachelor's degree in Communications with a Corporate Business / Public Relations focus, and Psychology, receiving an honors distinction.

In 2006, she graduated from the University of Michigan-Ann Arbor with a master's degree in Social Work. Her areas of study were Management of Human Services, and Community and Social Systems, with a minor in Community Organizing.

In 2009, she established "It's Time Enterprises." It is her motivational speaking company that is dedicated to empowering others to push beyond the barriers they encounter in life, in order to help them fulfill their dreams.

Following the establishment of this dynamic agency, Ms. Rice obtained a second master's degree in General Administration, and she received a Human Resource Administration certificate from Central Michigan University.

After completing her education, Ms. Rice created numerous products designed to help others improve their lives by changing their mindset and actions.

Some of these include creating a ringtone called "Thank You Haters," publishing the books "Gate to Life: You Choose the Life that You Shall Experience," and "Fruit Circle: Essential Fruit for Daily Living."

In 2020, she wrote the Forward to Glenn Murray et. al's book, "Faith, Failure, Success: Stories Along the Entrepreneurial

Journey," which became a Top 10 best-selling book on Amazon.

In 2021, she wrote a chapter in the book, "Faith, Failure, Success: Surviving the Storm," which also became a Top 10 best-selling book on Amazon.

Ms. Rice has spoken to large groups of youth and adults for more than 20 years. She is a licensed clinical social worker and has more than 20 years of experience counseling both youth and adults.

In addition, Ms. Rice has served as a delegate for Precinct 5 in the city of Westland, MI. She is the owner of a mindset coaching and clinical services provider known as Royal Clarity View LLC (RCV). Through this agency, she helps bereaved Christians regain hope by rediscovering their identity and healing through writing.

Upon completing the Royal Take-Over Program offered by RCV, each client experiences a mindset shift and publishes his or her story.

Further expanding her career, Ms. Rice is also the Director of Student Support Services and the Assistant Director of the Office of Trio Programs at the University of Michigan-Dearborn.Recently, she was certified by Chase Great University as a Mindset Coach. She also was a co-host of a broadcast show known as "Let's Talk About It 2.0."

Currently, she is writing several books, including "Hurt But Grateful," and "Living Diamonds," which will be released within the next two years.

To contact Ms. Rice or request a list of support system resources, email latresarice@royalclarityview.com or call 586-413-7158.